Math Fair Blues

by Sue Kassirer
Illustrated by Jerry Smath

The Kane Press
New York

For Laura
—S.K.

To Lauren Kleckner
—J.S.

Book Design/Art Direction: Roberta Pressel

Library of Congress Cataloging-in-Publication Data

Kassirer, Sue.
    Math fair blues/by Sue Kassirer; illustrated by Jerry Smath.
      p. cm. — (Math matters)
    Summary: Seth and his rock band perform at the school math fair and are surprised to find they are one of the prize winners.
    ISBN 1-57565-104-1 (pbk. : alk. paper)
    [1. Geometry—Fiction. 2. Schools—Fiction. 3. Musicians—Fiction.]
 I. Smath, Jerry, ill. II. Title. III. Series.

PZ7.K1562 Mat 2001
[E]—dc21

00-011405
CIP
AC

10 9 8 7 6 5 4 3 2 1

First published in the United States of America in 2001 by The Kane Press.
Printed in Hong Kong.

Talk about problems. Mine was called Math Fair, and it was just three days away. Guess who didn't have a project? Me. Neither did my friends. We were too busy with our new rock band... which gave me an idea!

"Could our band do a concert at the fair instead of a project?" I asked Mr. Wall the next day. "You know how you said that rhythm is kind of like math?"

"I sure did, Seth," Mr. Wall said. He thought hard. "Okay. You can play—but you still have to do math projects."

NEED HELP?
JUST ASK ME!

Mr. Wall

YIELD

BIKE PATH

LOOK AROUND !
2-Dimensional Shapes Are Everywhere

4/4

1,2,3,4   1,2,3,4

4

Our first real concert! My friends were excited too—but not about the math projects. The only one who didn't moan was Dana. Why would she? She gets all A's in math.

After school we rehearsed at Dana's.
"What will we wear?" she asked when
we were done. "And what about a name?"
Dana was right. We needed a name and
a look….We also needed a math project!

"Why don't we have T-shirts printed up with cool pictures?" said Jo.

"That would cost a fortune," Harry said, practicing his bow.

"I know!" said Dana. "We can print our own shirts with this kit I got for my birthday. Everyone just bring some white T-shirts over tomorrow."

"And ideas for designs," I said.

"And for math projects!" added Dana.

"Yeah, yeah," we all said.

The next day we started practicing on old shirts. It was good we did! Harry's guitar came out looking like a vase with a flower in it! Jo got more paint on the shirt she was wearing than on the one she was painting.

"I'm discouraged," Dana said. "Let's take a break."

"How about a snack?" said Jo. "Peanut butter and jelly always helps me think better."

It did help! Suddenly Jo cried out, "I've got it!" She washed the empty jelly jar and dipped it into the red paint. Then she pressed it onto her shirt. *Abracadabra!* A perfect red circle!

"Hey!" Dana shouted. "We could use other jars too—bigger ones, littler ones..."

"Why only use jars?" Harry said. "Look at all this stuff. We can print lots of shapes—triangles, squares, rectangles—whatever we can find."

"Well, not quite whatever," said Dana,
running over to me.

"Whoops!" I had picked up her mom's
best crystal vase.

"Look at this," said Dana. She was making a nice sharp print with a yellow block. It was just the shape I wanted— a rectangle. But I knew Dana. She'd be using it forever.

Ah-ha! I spotted a little plastic dollhouse. The bottom was the same size and shape as the block. Plus, it had a great handle!

Harry kept muttering, "Triangles would look cool. But I can't find a triangle shape." We all helped him look. It wasn't easy. The stuff we found was too big...

too breakable...

or too bumpy.

Dana saved the day. "Look!" she yelled. "This candy box is perfect!"

It *was* perfect. Harry used the top
for green triangles and the bottom for
yellow. And we all got to have another
snack.

"Hey, look!" cried Jo suddenly. She drew
a line across a square, from one corner to
the other. "Two triangles!" she said. "Am I
a genius, or what?"

Shapes were hiding out all over the place!

Finally we were done. And ask anyone. No fancy printer could have done a better job. The shirts looked great. "They're all different," Dana said. "But they all go together."

We got up early the next day for our
dress rehearsal. We sounded really good.
And Dana's dog made a great audience!

We were walking to school when it hit
me. "Oh, no!" I said. "We forgot about
the math projects!"

"Uh, oh," said Harry and Jo.

"Too late now," said Dana. "I just hope
Mr. Wall still lets us perform!"

But that morning Mr. Wall had his mind on something else. A surprise quiz—in math! Just my luck, I thought. My worst subject. I have no project. And now a test!

But guess what the test was on? 2-D
shapes—just like the ones on our shirts!
The four of us winked at one another.
Guess what again? I knew all the answers!

GUESS WHAT?
QUIZ TODAY!
2-DIMENSIONAL SHAPES
SQUARE   TRIANGLE   CIRCLE   RECTANGLE

Next thing we knew, it was time to set up the math projects.

"Let's get out of here," Harry whispered. "Mr. Wall might forget about us if he doesn't see us."

Quickly, we made a beeline for the auditorium.

We hid backstage until our big moment.

25

Finally the curtain opened.

"Welcome!" said the principal, Mrs. Phillips. "Before I present the awards, we have a special surprise—our own student rock band, the...uh..." She looked at us.

MATH FAIR AWARDS

"We forgot to name the band!" Jo whispered.

"On top of forgetting the math projects," said Dana.

Someone had to do something—quick. So I grabbed the mike and called out, "The 2-D Rockers!" The audience clapped like mad, and we began to play.

They loved us! The clapping went on
and on and on. Mrs. Phillips had to
shush everybody so she could give out
the awards.

As soon as we sat down, I stopped feeling like a rock star. I was a regular kid again—a kid with no math project.

I got really nervous. I didn't hear a thing until Mrs. Phillips said, "And now for our last award. It's brand new, and it's for the Most Artistic Math Project. It goes to…

"The 2-D Rockers, for their T-shirt math project!"

Math project? Award? Us? We couldn't believe it! We had won an award in the Math Fair!

The audience yelled, "Encore! Encore!" So we played again. And one thing was for sure—the 2-D Rockers were in great shape!

2-D SHAPES CHART

Here are some 2-dimensional shapes.

Find the shapes that are **congruent.**

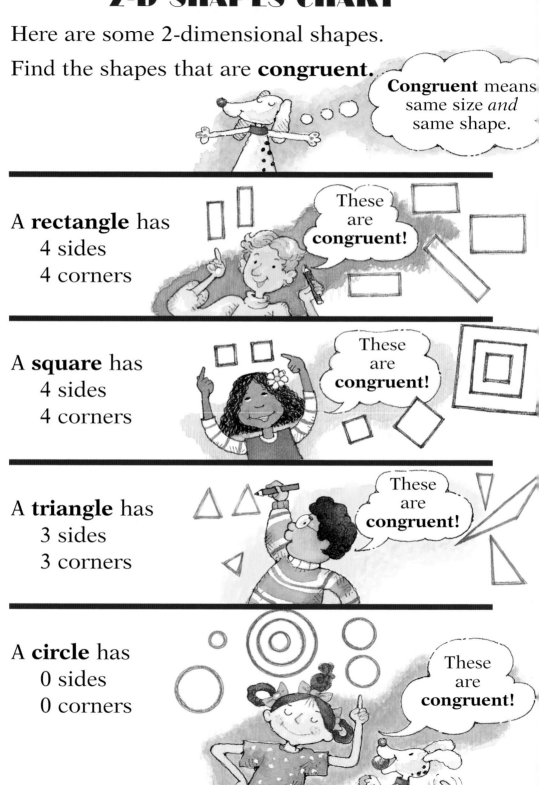

Congruent means same size *and* same shape.

A **rectangle** has
  4 sides
  4 corners

These are **congruent!**

A **square** has
  4 sides
  4 corners

These are **congruent!**

A **triangle** has
  3 sides
  3 corners

These are **congruent!**

A **circle** has
  0 sides
  0 corners

These are **congruent!**